Duck's Easter Egg Hunt

DUCK'S EASTER EGG HUNT
First published in Great Britain by Picture Corgi, an imprint of Random House Children's Publishers UK
A Random House Group Company

ISBN 978-1-4351-5243-4

Manufactured in China
Lot #:
2 4 6 8 10 9 7 5 3
10/14

Duck's Easter Egg Hunt

Dawn Richards
& Heidi D'hamers

Sandy Creek
NEW YORK

The village was full of excitement as everyone prepared for the Easter parade.

Hedgehog had baked some chocolate muffins,

Mole had learned a special Easter song,

Cat had made some
Easter cakes,

Rabbit was decorating an Easter
float with garlands of spring flowers.
And Duck . . .

Duck was more excited than anyone else.
Her precious egg was very nearly ready to hatch.
What would she do while she waited?

Through the window, Duck spied her friend Rabbit's children playing in the garden. There were three little bunnies –

Floppy,

Poppy

and Hoppy!

Seeing them gave Duck a great idea . . .

"I'll organize an Easter egg hunt!" Duck flapped happily.
"I'll decorate some eggs and hide them for the children
to find."

One by one she painted beautiful patterns on some eggs.

She painted stripy patterns, spotty patterns, and zigzaggy patterns.
As she painted, Duck looked lovingly at her own precious egg.

Once the eggs were decorated, Duck carefully loaded them into her big basket and set out to hide them, with a waddle and a quack.

She hid eggs here,

she hid eggs there.

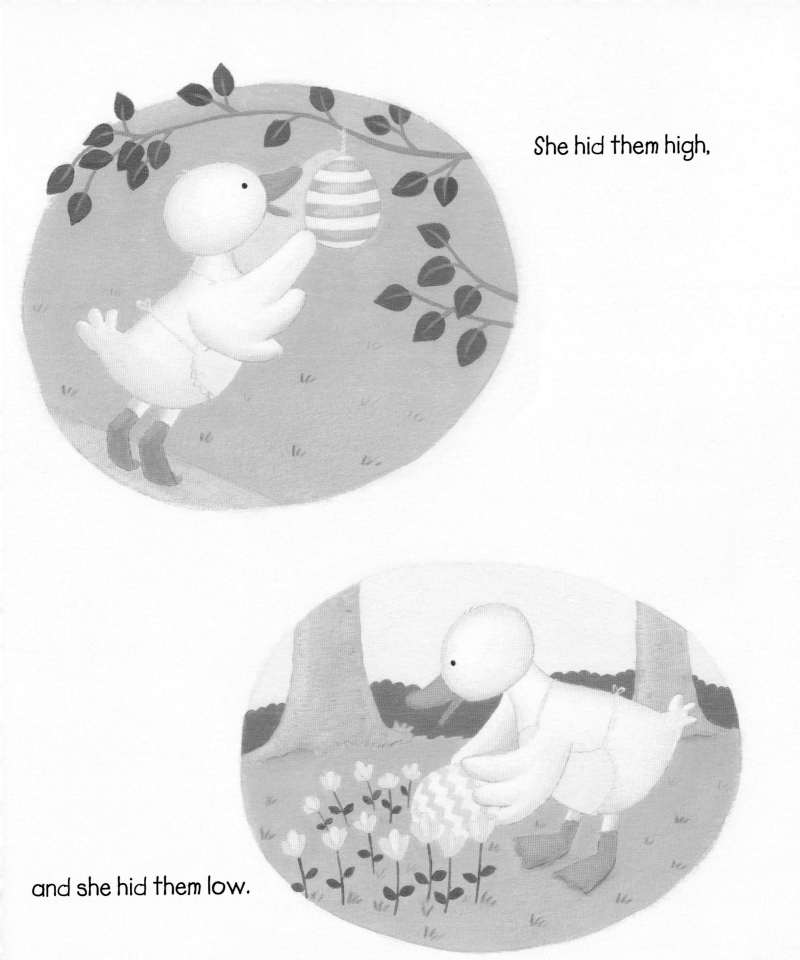

She hid them high,

and she hid them low.

But Duck was so distracted, thinking about all the Easter celebrations ahead, that she accidentally hid her own precious egg . . .

Oh no, Duck!

It was only when she got home that she realized:

"MY PRECIOUS EGG
- IT'S GONE!"

Duck simply could not remember where she had hidden her egg.
"I'm such a very silly Duck," she quacked miserably,
tears rolling down her beak.

Her friends all tried to make her feel better. "Come on, Duck,"
said Rabbit. "My little bunnies will help you find your egg
- we'll all do it together!"

So, Hedgehog took the bunnies to look down by the lake.

"I spy one egg," said Hoppy.

"I can spot two," shouted Floppy.

"I can see three,"
whooped Poppy.

But there was no sign of Duck's egg.

"I can find three," whooped Hoppy.

But there was still not a trace of Duck's egg.

Finally, Cat took the bunnies to search in the forest.

"I spy one egg," said Poppy.

"I can see two," shouted Hoppy.

"I can find three," whooped Floppy.

But where, oh where, was Duck's precious egg?

Duck was so sad and worried. "My poor precious egg!"
she snuffled.

"Calm down, Duck," said Hedgehog, who was secretly a little bit worried himself. "Where else did you hide the eggs?"

"Well," Duck sniffed, "I think I hid the last eggs in Rabbit's garden . . ."

The friends rushed to Rabbit's garden, where they hunted high and low.
Suddenly . . .

"I spy one,"
shouted Floppy.

"I spy one,
yelled Pop

"I spy one,"
whooped Hoppy.

"And I spy one!" quacked Duck.
She had found her precious egg.

Floppy was happy
- he had six stripy
eggs.

Hoppy was happy
- he had six spotty
eggs.

And Poppy was happy
- she had six zigzaggy
eggs.

But Duck was the happiest of all -
she had one very precious egg . . .

that was just about
to hatch.

Quack!

Duck and her new baby joined the Easter parade to celebrate Little Duck's first ever Easter . . .

Happy

...and Duck's best Easter ever!

The End